W9-BLB-163

First published by Parragon in 2013
Parragon
Chartist House
15–17 Trim Street
Bath BA1 1HA, UK
www.parragon.com

Copyright © 2013 Disney Enterprises, Inc.

Edited by: Gemma Louise Lowe
Designed by: Joe Scott
Production by: Jack Aylward

All rights reserved. No part of this publication may be reproduced, stored in a retrieval system or transmitted, in any form or by any means, electronic, mechanical, photocopying, recording or otherwise, without the prior permission of the copyright holder.

ISBN 978-1-78186-862-1

Printed in China

MICKEY MOUSE
AND HIS FRIENDS

Bath • New York • Singapore • Hong Kong • Cologne • Delhi
Melbourne • Amsterdam • Johannesburg • Shenzhen

A Christmas party at Mickey's house
Was a signal for bundles of fun,
And all the gang arrived with gifts,
Which were opened one by one.

Oh boy, oh boy! Was Donald cross!
He almost had a fright,
Then stormed and ranted around the room,
And quacked: "Ya wanna fight?"

Horace is so full of pride
That he will use up his last dollar
For a picture of a handsome pair,
Himself and his collar!

The cuckoo clock that Goofy got,
Popped out and laid him flat!
It would have knocked him silly
But he was already that!

Christmas bells for Clarabelle Cow
Will ring through the year with grace,
For she'll be stepping out in style,
With her new electric necklace.

**Cat-chaser Pluto grinned and said:
"I'd rather chase 'em, but—aw, rats!
I can't today, because it's Christmas!
Peace on earth and good will to cats!"**

The Orphans' gift—a book of tricks—
Delights them. But we fear
The weather will be pretty bad
For ducks, this coming year!

MERRY XMAS
FOR
MINNIE MOUSE

Minnie surely liked her hat—
It looked so cute and chic and tricky—
Made by Monsieur Michel Moussé!
(Which—we hope—is French for "Mickey"!)

The new band leader's uniform
For Mickey makes a hit.
He'll look real sharp when he puts it on,
To that we must admit!

The Pigs got a break from Santa;
They're set for a season at least.
All safe from the claws
Of that old wolf, because
They're harder to catch when they're greased.

THE END

CLOCK CLEANERS

One day, Donald Duck was a little bored because nothing much was happening. So, he thought he would go and see what his friend, Mickey Mouse, was doing.

When he reached Mickey's house, he walked in and called out, "Oh, Mickey!"

Mickey came down from the attic, where he was doing some housecleaning.

"Hello, old pal. Glad to see you! Step right in!" said Mickey.

"I thought I might help you," said Donald, reluctantly.

"That's swell," replied Mickey as they went upstairs.
"Here's a broom ... or would you prefer a duster?"

Before Donald had a chance to change his mind, Mickey put a
duster in his hands. Mickey thought that he would try to blow
the dust away first.

Most of the dust flew straight into Donald's face! It made a mess everywhere, so Mickey and Donald had to get busy mopping and dusting.

They scrubbed and swept until the attic began to look pretty tidy. Donald soon began searching for something more interesting to do.

"Say, Mickey, how about that old grandfather clock in the corner?
Don't you think it needs cleaning?" asked Donald.

"I guess so. I bet it would work if we just gave it a good scrub,"
said Mickey, glancing at the old clock. No sooner than that was said,
Donald and Mickey set to work.

Mickey got a large bucket of water, and Donald put some soap suds in it, which made a bucket of soapy suds.

Then, Mickey got the scrubbing brush and Donald took the mop, and between them, they washed the clock hands and face until they shone.

Then, they scrubbed the rest of the clock.

Next, they dried it thoroughly and then Donald dusted off the cogs inside.

"There sure are a lot of parts to this clock," said Donald, as he tried to put them back together again. He worked away on the clock and soon had several parts back in place.

Or at least, he thought they were in place....

"I wonder what to do with all the parts that are left over,"
thought Donald. "I guess I'd better just throw them in. I'm sure
they'll just fall into place."

Mickey gathered the remaining pieces, and Donald just dropped
them into the body of the clock. Mickey gave them an approving
pat, while Donald took a look at the cuckoo.

"You need some feathers," Donald said to the cuckoo. "You look quite bare." He pulled out a fine, large feather from the feather duster.

"This will make you quite handsome," he said, as he stuck the plume where the cuckoo's tail should have been.

Mickey oiled the cogs, and then the clock was finished!

"I think it looks nice enough to put downstairs in the hallway," said Mickey. "Let's surprise Minnie!"

"I'll wind it up and you call her," said Donald.

So, Mickey went to call Minnie and Donald started winding the clock.

Suddenly, Mickey heard the most startling noises. He rushed back to Donald.

"Bang! Crash!"

The clock fell to the floor in pieces! Minnie heard the crash and rushed upstairs.

"What have you done to my clock?" she cried.

"We'll buy you a new one," promised Mickey.

"Well, next time you want to clean a clock," said Minnie, "be sure to take it to the watch repair shop!"